Published by Jaded Ibis Press, *sustainable literature by digital means*™, an
imprint of Jaded Ibis Productions, LLC, Seattle, Washington USA.

Rachel May. Cover and book design by Debra Di Blasi.

This book is available in multiple formats, including multimedia. Visit
our website for more information: jadedibisproductions.com

OUT FROM THE PLEIADES

A PICARESQUE NOVELLA IN VERSE

LESLIE McGRATH

Jaded Ibis Press
sustainable literature by digital means™
an imprint of Jaded Ibis Productions
Seattle • Hong Kong • Boston

"All cruelty springs from weakness."

—Seneca

"Let a man get up and say, Behold, this is the truth, and instantly I see a sandy cat filching a piece of fish in the background. Look, you have forgotten the cat, I say."

—Virginia Woolf

TABLE OF CONTENTS

We Come upon Mina

The crowded mountains she's driven down
                              jaggedly down
like a crack in porcelain
                              now seem a huddle
                              of distant cattle.

          The road jigged right
                              at a white clapboard church
& once she passed over
                    the temporary bridge
          that every car knocks the wind out of
                    she found a mill   (old wood, new paint)
                              & parked.

Here   Mina in her black down coat
                    down to the tops
          of her small black boots
     stood smoking
          cigarette after cigarette
                    lighting one
                         from the other

          furiously   furiously   furious.

                    College was turning out
                    to be a monumental bore
                    & the exercise of free speech
                    was often a bust.

Mina—   born at the lip of a bullhorn
       & at the tail
           of a political age
      was taught to speak her mind & speak it loudly

              she raised her voice
more often than most students   raise their hands
more often than parishioners   raise their hearts.

Get out of Afghanistan, Imperialist pawns!

This she hissed at a counterful of soldiers
      breakfasting at a dingy diner
           near Westover Air Force base.

    With a swiftness she hadn't counted on
        one rushed at her full-on,
  the top of his head hitting Mina's solar plexus
        like a battering ram at a drum skin.

      Bent like a pin, she fell
      into the arms of another uniform
        —a woman with uncommon
           golden eyes—
    who spun her toward the door, rasping,
       Please get out
      before you get hurt.

As she   eased   behind   the wheel
    of her battered Subaru   Mina glimpsed her petite savior
                       blocking the exit
                       & behind that camo'ed arm
      the lunging, livid faces
      of various military personnel.

     Was it a ringing in her ears she heard?
        All in all it was
        just another brick in the wall.

These words clanged through Mina
like dumb electricity
as she played her fingers over her ribs.

She felt pain but
where was the wound?

Crushing the cigarette underheel
she watched her tobacco plume rise   rise
past the topmost branches
of the white pines
past steepletop & contrail
past stratosphere

toward the Pleiades.

Our Heroine is Born & Brings Dinner

She raged forth from the dark red dark

> & slid into the family tub
> amid the cheers of a welcoming tribe
> of women
> who called themselves the Seven Sisters.

With a yellow-checked tea towel
they rubbed the breath into her
as they rubbed off
the slick of her journey

> & wrapped her like a baguette.

Mina   said her mother   *She must be Mina Kali*

Naming is making   & here was a name
that sat like a crown
on her soft little head
but despite its grand sound

Mina is Sanskrit for *fish*   & Kali's the goddess of destruction.

> A piranha
> couldn't be better named.

It was the month of topaz & thanks.
                    The tom turkey in the yard had become
                        an apple-fattened menace
                            rushing the fencing
                                meant to confine him.

He held his warty head with the jaunty hauteur of the doomed.

        & the leaves of the beech   *yellow yellow yellow*
                                                hushed
                                            in their falling....

    while up under the eaves
        her mother gave a final
        sour-breathed heave
                                            as Mina napped
            a swaddled storm in an auntie's arms
                        & the ruby placenta
                            slopped
                        into an old bread bowl
        (its gold glaze crazed from years of use)
        & was swiftly delivered
        downstairs to the round kitchen table.

            Mutterkuchen.   Mother-cake.

The Seven Sisters had delivered them before.
                Midwives all
            except for Auntie Anna   the cook
                                    who entered the bodies
                                    of the Sisters & their children
                                through the work of her hands
                                as peeler, stirrer, kneader, baker.

            So they partook
            of her good will
            & Mina's placenta

because the Maori do
because the Navajo do
because goats & camels do
because it is *natural*
                    though with cups of green tea
                                            & a toast

                            to family unity.

Auntie Anna's Placenta Stew

After you wash the placenta, pat it dry and scrape away the membrane.
Let it rest while you stir a mixture of flour (half white, half wheat), a pinch of salt
    and a few grinds of pepper in a pie plate.
Cut the placenta into bite-sized pieces and toss them into the flour mixture.
Once they're coated, put them aside to dry; dice celery, carrots and onion.
Slowly cook this trinity in olive oil, and when the onions give up their opacity, add
    a handful of sliced mushrooms—wild, if you can find them.
Let the mushrooms release their liquid, and once they have, add the placenta.
Let the placenta brown companionably with vegetables for a few minutes.
Now is the time to add something acidic— a can of tomatoes or a couple glugs of wine.
Pick a handful of herbs, thyme for strength, rosemary for ardor, basil for balance.
Toss these atop the stew and cover it with a loose-fitting lid.
Set the table, clean the kitchen, and when you're ready, the stew will be too.

Mina's Childhood Leaves an Impression

Mina's first three years
                    were spent as close as
                              close is
              to the two other children
              of the group of women
              who'd been together   since the early 70's
                              (a/k/a ancient times)
                              at UNH.

        In a nest of patched quilts & pillows
                    sour-sweet with their spit-up
                              set up
                              like a whelping basket
                              next to the woodstove
              they played, napped
          & occasionally pulled hair
      while the beat of 70's mix tapes
      lub-dubbed in the background   as a kind of aural wallpaper.

  The children were

      Abby   Abenaki Indian   who the aunties had fostered since birth
      Mina   homemade   thanks to an unsuspecting semen donor
      & Malcolm   half white/ half black who the aunties called African American
                                          adopted at 3 months.

    To the Seven Sisters   America was a place of violence & injustice
                              also a place of opportunity &plenty
          so they took one child
          from each of the ethnic groups
              that interested them most.

Abby   eldest
   walked first

         leaving Mina & Malcolm
            creeping far behind
           often grasping
         for the same handhold
    on the wobbly kitchen chairs
       & creaky stairs
      that led to the bedrooms.

Ambulation earned Abby
   first choice of bedrooms
       but instead of taking
      the largest or sunniest
    Abby chose the nook closest
          to the wing where her aunties slept.

Once all three children
were walking & talking   they were deemed
            ready for schooling
    down in the cellar classroom
      where a ravaged blackboard
      & five mustard-yellow vinyl chairs
           snagged in a Sunday scavenge
     from the dumpster   behind a Midas muffler shop
      were arranged in a sacred circle.

From behind a saggy batiked screen
   the old washing machine
    chomped & slurped
  through its weekly cuisine.

This was where the aunties taught the children   everything
                                                                                    (they thought)
                                                                                    the children needed
                                                                                    to know.

          The necessaries   (alphabet, colors & simple math)
                              were taught from the same primers
                                        the aunties had been taught from—

          Dick & Jane ran
          & watched Spot run
                    across the thick pages
                    worn soft & gray as moleskin

                                        though Jane's hair was a bit darker
                                                            a bit curlier
                                        her skin benefitted from
                                                  the bronzing melanin
                              of Auntie Jean's ocher Sharpie pen

          (with which she'd chastely edited "Dick"
                              to "Richard.")

Only the Best: A Homemade Scrapbook Primer

The Seven Sisters pooled their expertise
 & found (though it was no surprise to them)
the curriculum in Portsmouth public schools
from kindergarten through the seventh grade
was a ghoulish goulash of misdirected myth—
a litany of skirmishes in swamps
from Maine to Washington, then *westward ho!*
The wagon trains, brute Injuns & the Gold Rush
just a rush to conquer nature, kill the beast
called wilderness. Success—it's wild no more.

The great Midwest's now choked with factory farms
their noxious runoff poisoning the wells.
Monsanto, greedy pitchfork-shaking Satan,
who foisted GMO on soy and corn—
was barely mentioned in New Hampshire texts.
What's next? Omit the fact that Uncle Sam
sold weapons to Iran, Afghanistan?

You could fill a book from those lacunae.
so fill they did— called it their scrapbook primer.
No wars allowed, their textbook spotlit lives
of heroes like Thoreau & Emerson
John Reed & Emma Goldman, socialists
& certain suffragettes, then moving on
to Civil Rights & strangely, the Space Race
(Auntie Nan's obsession), climate change.
They pasted articles from *Mother Jones*,
The Nation, Utne Reader, their local rag—
the venerable *New Hampshire Gazette*,
"the nation's oldest newspaper"™

They bound a dozen copies of these books
with silver plumber's tape in hope that word
would spread from Portsmouth outward to the world.
They'd welcome other classmates so their three
 would have companions. This was not to be.

The Homeschool Curriculum

On the first day
of the first year   of their formal education
the first assignment   was a self-portrait

Abby, Mina & Malcolm
drew with the black pens
given them

head hair eyes mouth neck body arms legs..... *ta-da!*

then each was handed
a thick crayon
of the appropriate hue—

"Indian Red" for Abby
(since renamed "Chestnut")
"Flesh" for Mina
(since renamed "Peach")
"Gray" for Malcolm
(a darker tone, "Outer Space"
was introduced years later by the manufacturer.)

Once they colored themselves in
the children were ready for filling
like Auntie Anna's pie crusts.

From their small circle
in the classroom
each child could see duct-taped to the concrete walls
a poster of a hero—

fierce Che   in his black beret
Dr. King   peering through his "I Have a Dream" speech
Angela Davis   cool & defiant

& a poster of "the Movement"——

a tie-died peace banner that had twice marched on Washington
(with a couple of burns from dropped joints
which the children thought
were bullet holes)

a copy of Elizabeth Cady Stanton's <u>Declaration of Sentiments</u>
signed by the women at Seneca Falls.

& a poster that declared:

**It'll be a great day
when our day care centers
have all the money they need
and the Navy has to hold a bake sale
to buy battleships.**

The First Hints of Mina's Remarkable Aptitude

It was an August so hot & dry
                    the grasshoppers could not   stop   leaping.

                              Each stalk of Indian paintbrush
    (which the children were told to call   Native American paintbrush)
        was orange-burnt   an ember
                    on a poker.

It was a summer stingy with dew—
                    on the days it beaded the grass
            the sun shone so fierce on those convexities
                              it burned the green blades brown
            on the spots where the dew sat
                    before   evaporating.

    Those speckled grasses
                    were good cover
            for all manner of hoppers
                    & a challenge for Mina to catch.

    She needed food for her pet garter snake
                    live food.
            She enjoyed watching
                        the snake's casual outcurling
            & the stunned   useless kicking
                    of its prey.

Mina wondered
why the insects never saw it coming.

                              After all
                              they were alone
                              in a tank
                              with a snake.

Easygoing Malcolm & Independent Abby

Malcolm   the youngest
                        was happy to catch grasshoppers
        while Mina read in the shade   so eager to be near her
                            he'd do whatever she asked
                            he'd fetch her lemonade
                            he'd do her tasks.

    Abby   had talented hands
                agreed the aunties   delighted.
                    They'd read
                            of her tribe's stitchery
                & hoped
                            to encourage a propensity
                for the needle's deft conversation.

        So Abby   hemmed the pants & dresses
                        bought on Bag Day
                                at the Portsmouth Good Will
                    kept up the button can & the rag bag
                    made change purses for Christmas gifts.

She knitted, appliquéd, crotcheted & bargelloed
                        her way into every auntie's heart.

Mina watched   Abby's fleet fingers
                    her quiet focus
                    her patience   & understood
                            that by making things
                            Abby made herself
                            valuable.

        But Abby's kindness
                felt like a kind of sloppiness—
                like one of Auntie Nan's

leaky kisses
after she finished another bottle
of Auntie Anna's May wine—
                    its oozy ways worked against
                    the *us-versus-them* designations
                with which Mina had grown
                            so comfortable.

One cool Saturday afternoon
as she chose smooth stones from the driveway
     for the cairn she was constructing
    in her snake's tank
        Mina made up a song:

> *Abby, Abby, what does she know?*
>   *How to quilt and how to sew.*
> *Abby, Abby, who is her friend?*
>   *Nobody. All she does is mend.*
> *Abby, Abby, needle & thread.*
>   *She'll sew & sew until she's dead.*

When Malcolm asked to play
    with Mina that day   the price
        was learning the song
        which Malcolm chanted gleefully
        under the flapping paisley sheets
            pinned on the clothesline
        hung from pine to sugar maple.

He didn't see Auntie Karen
    the disciplinarian
        & laundry goddess   lay her wicker basket down
  & stand
    hands on ample hips

        while Malcolm's pure soprano
          rang out
      the chorus for a third time.

When he was done
    he was done for—
      Auntie Karen laid into him
        & sent the boy to his room
          without supper.

      At the table that night
      over tempeh tostadas
      a discussion was had
      about the inevitability
      of male aggression.

Further Details on the Children's Education

As in most matters
   the Seven Sisters   decided by committee
            how to educate their children.

    There were Spanish lessons & painting lessons
          social sciences & math
           but English was tricky   (Mina never forgot
                           the arguments about
                           "The Cannon.")

The children had been taught which words
                  to omit
                  from the Pledge of Allegiance
  & were frankly discouraged
    from singing
    The Star Spangled Banner

        (its glaring rockets & bursting bombs
          were too militaristic
          declared Auntie Sarah
          the group's U.S. history maven.)

Etiquette of a sort
was also taught
    but not the "please pass the peas"
        no boardinghouse reach
        "yes Ma'am" "No Sir"
        manners hammered
        into generations of children.

           The aunties' priority?
           A full-voiced *Speak Truth to Power*
           attitude in their three. Along with a firm handshake
           & the understanding that if arrested a march
           or demonstration (which constituted much of their
           family's social life) all that goes out the window:
                        Go limp.

Mina Begins to Have Questions

I have seven moms.
        Who is my dad?

If all whites are racist
          am I racist too?

Why didn't I get a Barbie Dreamhouse for Christmas?

If the police & government can't be trusted
               why trust my aunties?

I have seven moms.
        Who is my dad?

If religion is for morons
             why do we recite Reverend King
             each morning before our muesli?

Why can't I wear my pink tutu outside the house?

If everyone is equal
        why is President Reagan so bad?

Who is my dad?

Abby Blossoms in Middle School

When each child moved into a second decade
        she or he was sent   to the local middle school
                                        down the mountain
      along with Auntie Emily   a 6th grade math teacher.

       After a breakfast
        of whole oats
        brewer's yeast
        & blackstrap molasses
            (Adelle Davis still had her ghostly finger
                        in the family cuisine)
Abby would dress
make herself an almond butter sandwich
    on Auntie Anna's homemade bread
        & wait at the back door
      darning a mitten
      or fixing a rip with a decorative stitch
                until it was time to leave.

                        Rather, she'd be
                        re-crocheting
                        & re-fixing.

    It seemed she'd never finished
    as much as she thought she had.

  From 7:25am to 2:05pm
    each weekday
    Abby excelled.
              She was grades ahead
         in reading
              & though quiet
       she was known to be
            quite kind.

             But on weekends & evenings
               Abby occupied a territory

between
ignored & besieged.
She'd return home to board games in progress
games that lasted days
& which she was not allowed to join
because
"it's not right to start something in the middle."

Imperialism
the family's favorite
had been cobbled together
from a Monopoly board:

the familiar Atlantic City landmarks
replaced with global real estate destinations
well-known for their struggles
against various Imperialisms
through the ages.

Boardwalk & Park Place   became Hong Kong
Mediterranean & Baltic Avenues   were Africa
India   occupied the entire railroad system
the utilities   served as the Phillippines
& everyone agreed that Chance best suited Puerto Rico.

She or he who returned the most money
was declared the winner.

Not that there weren't disputes.

Auntie Karen, a nonpracticing Jew
was so upset
when the rest
voted in the Golan Heights
that she "forgot"
to put the yeast
in her bread that week.

Up the stairs Abby would trudge
     to her nook
         tucked up against the aunties' wing
   with a snack
            (a whole oat muffin
            spread with apple butter
            or her favorite kale chips)
      curl up on her bed
    & do her homework
        using the required #2 pencil
         & find the next morning
               random answers   erased.

        Abby took this in stride
           mystified
   & because she was a stubborn one
     began to do homework in pen.

A Small Private Satisfaction

Sipping milky tea
from her yellow mug
Mina smiled; it took
only five minutes
to unravel the sleeve

Abby had knitted
for Auntie Sarah's
fiftieth birthday.

Abby & Mina in Middle School

Mina followed Abby
to the public middle school
after seventh grade

where Abby had established herself
as a person who did for others—

she was a guider of wheelchairs
a tutor of English for the refugees
from Sudan
who'd been sent unluckily
to chilly New England
& an afterschool helper
of the beleaguered part-time custodian.

For teachers & staff   this was reason to smile.
For Mina   this was provocation.

Rumors began to circulate—   that Abby was being paid
for her kindnesses

that Abby was a shoplifter
recently released
from reform school.

Mina reassured Abby's friends:
Oh no, Abby never shoplifted!
But she almost grew up
in a reform school 'cuz her whole family
were crazy drunks
& then my aunties took her in.

Abby's friends, stunned
didn't quite believe the stories
but it was a bit
more difficult
to fit

her
at their lunch table

& a bit
easier
to forget
to invite her
to their sleepovers.

Abby faded from their attention.....

But Mina
oh Mina they noticed

when she held her nose each time Ms. Thompson
whose putrid breath
came from bad dental health
passed by her desk

when she'd toss Ginger Chew's lunch
into the garbage can
chirping
"Ginger can't chew today."

& when she'd hang inside the door
of the beautiful Ms. Singh
repeating the same lame joke
"Shouldn't you be
a chorus teacher
not an English teacher?"
Then Ms. Singh would smile
& squeeze Mina's shoulder
& just for a moment
something in Mina
would loosen
& soften.

One Morning in the Principal's Office
at Portsmouth High

—*You know why you're here, don't you? Your home room teacher sent you down because he doesn't know what to do with you. Why can't you stand with the others, just stand there while the Pledge is being said? You don't have to put your hand over your heart. Just stand there respectfully. Out of respect for your fellow students if not the flag. But I do have to say, Mina, you're not winning any friends with this kind of behavior.*

We Meet Mina's Target

Ginger Chew was an awkward girl
but there are few things less elegant
than a thirteen year old.

Even Lacey MacNeil
student council president
soccer star & an overbrimming 36C
came to school with hair so oily
toward the end of the week   that when she moved
suddenly
the acrid mosquito-buzz stink of her hair
floated, fartlike,
through American history class.

Ginger's glandularity was no worse
than Lacey's
or Mina's
her clothes no cooler
her grades no better

but Ginger had a habit
of biting her nails
down to their bleeding quicks.

That she did this in class
this intimate practice
in front of her peers
in the kind of reverie reserved for, say
nose-picking
infuriated Mina—
Gross! What's wrong with her!
Doesn't Ginger know
you do certain things
in private?

Mina hatched a plan.

Dear students of Mr. Washington's 5th period English class,

We are pleased to announce a food drive for our fellow student, Ginger Chew. It has come to our atention that Ginger desparatly needs food so she can keep growing!! Please save all your nail clippings from fingers and toes from now until after winter vacation. Ginger cannot live without them!!

From The Crew To Feed Ginger Chew

(The CTFGC)

Mina   who'd been taught to follow through
                                    followed through—

     she saved her nail clippings   finger & toe
          in a discarded amber vial
               after scratching off her mother's name
                    & the word *Clonazepam.*

                                        (As she pawed
                              through the bathroom trash
                         she found a bounty
                         of other clippings
                         & dropped them into the nail vial.
                         This became her weekly practice.)

Behind the whitewashed clapboards of a dozen Portsmouth houses
behind the bathroom doors of Portsmouth's best addresses
two dozen students saved their filthy sickle-shaped clippings
in a kind of viral violence that thrilled Mina, teen oppressor.

History is Made in American History Class

Ladies & Gentlemen
      & esteemed readers from all parts
   local & far-flung

        on this, the eighth day of January
          Miss Ginger Chew will be honored with

               A LIFETIME SUPPLY

           of the cream of the crop   the top of the heap
                the most delicious   nutritious
              fungus-riddled rinds   it has been Mina's pleasure to collect!

This is a truly stupendous   life-changing
                gift   wrapped
                     in expensive embossed silver paper
                     saved since last Christmas by none other than
              Abby   who had been pleaded with
                     cajoled & finally bought outright
          with a promise   that Mina would do her chores
                     for the week.

      For an extra week off
          from doing the dishes
           & scooping the litter
    Abby wrapped the shifty little box

                    which Ginger discovered
                    resting jauntily on her desk
                    in history class
                    on the Monday after Christmas break.

        Yes, Ladies & Gentlemen
          she opened it
          she opened it so quickly
          & with such high-pitched zeal

that they who did their best
to look elsewhere
to avoid implication
gasped along with Ginger
when the contents of the box
seemed to explode   sending thousands of clippings
                                     sharp   yellowing   shrapnel
                                     onto Ginger   & her neighbors

"Alright Ginger, very funny.
Wipe off your desk.
We've got lots to get to today."   With that, Mr. Washington
                                        launched into his lecture
                                        on Reagan's efforts to unite
                                        the two Germanys.
                                        "Tear down that wall, Mr. Gorbachev!"

            All in all it's just
            another brick in the wall.....

What a chorus, Ladies & Gentlemen, what a moment!

On her long walk home that day
Ginger's breath as it left her lips
became a wheaten bale of shame
tumbling in the weak winter light.

High School: an ode to accretion

It
begins
with a zit
a spray of zits
pus buckshot
bra straps & tits
fried eggs, skeeter bites
cantelopes & headlights
he's got a boner, a stiffy
 a woody, a chubby, a hard-on
she's on the rag, riding a tampon
she's got the curse, the crimson tide, aunt Flo's
visiting, he's rank, he stinks, she's stank, a skanky ho
she's trailer trash, he's nascar, a cracker, a redneck, a hick
that's so gay, she's bi, a rug muncher, a dyke, a lipstick lesbian
he's a faggot, a fairy, a homo, queer, brokeback, light in the loafers, a limp dick
they're lame, losers, tools, dorks, douchebags, morons, pussies, retards & fucktards all.

Everyone Faces a Wall Sometime

By the time the tuxes were rented
               & the local florist's fingers
                    were blistered from twisting
                         the stems
             of 206 chrysanthemum corsages
                in Portsmouth High's   yellow & purple
      each of the Seven Sisters' children
                    had a plan
   & each   met a wall
               which blocked that plan.

                   Abby's wish to major in fiber arts at RISD
                      was thwarted by family finances.
                     She would take a year off
                        then two   then five
                          & live at home
                  (in fact she'd never leave)
              saving her paycheck   waiting
                               tables
                 at a local Greek diner
                 & teach weaving
              in continuing ed. classes.

Mina was accepted
by every college
she'd applied to
on the strength
of her SAT analytical score
              & though she intended
                to major in the arts
                the only promise she showed
            was an increasing subtlety
               in the art of
               humiliation:

she'd learned to disguise
her distinctive low voice
during late-night calls
to Ginger's cell phone
asking for appointments
for a mani-pedi &
complimentary massage.

When came his time
to graduate from Portsmouth High
Malcolm   co-captain of the basketball team
who led them to victory
in the New Hampshire state finals
was UNH's #1 recruit.

Malcolm would go on
to make his coaches proud
though he succumbed
to the full court press
of seven determined aunties

(who did not raise a young black man
to become something as racially cliché
as a professional basketball player)

& majored in political science
struggling through economics
both macro & micro
with the help of a tutor.

He would go on
to a steady but unexciting career
as a loan officer
at Portsmouth Savings Bank
spending evenings & weekends
doing what he loved—

coaching the local YMCA basketball team.

Mina on the Bridge

Mina believed she'd never seen otters or mink;
though auntie Jean's car had rumbled over a corpse

one late December afternoon   & Mina thought she knew
the torn bag of fur and gut had once been muskrat.

For days the thermometer's needle had not passed zero.
Mina stopped mid-cross on the footbridge over the river

 to watch two brown commas   (otter   mink   or muskrat?)
race along the icecoast   up deep banks made deeper by snow

& roll down   chittering   into a river   half ice, half water.
Mina wondered whether this was play or war

whether these beasts were grown or growing.
Crossings are their most opaque when we're halfway through.

So she named them mink & called it war
but they were pups at play   & otters.

Mina Attends Vassar

Leave it up to a child   & the decision's made
                              through a rope course of tangents
                                   (& a few unconscious loop de loos)

Mina choice of Vassar   one of the Seven Sisters colleges
                              (also the nick for the Pleiades
                                   whose stars
                                   wink in the winter heavens
                              & in whom Mina always saw an arrow in flight)

was a source of amusement & relief to the aunties
     who had been stumped by Mina's antics
     & had a vague sense of guilt
     they explained away
     through her father's probable
          genetic shortcomings.

Mina studied   Plath Virgil Derrida
     played   beer pong chess viola
     observed   Kwanzaa Earth Day Ramadan.

          She gave up   Cheez Doodles   white food
                    & eating anything with eyelashes.

She protested America's corporate culture
          by forgoing toothpaste   shampoo   & deodorant.

She saved water by not doing laundry
    & following the *if it's yellow* edict.

        Thus Mina's consciousness expanded   expanded
                  & again expanded
    until her roommate grew intolerable
        then the other students
   & even her professors
     except Dr. Randolph
        who was   intolerable to begin with.

Eventually Mina avoided
    the public spaces
    the libraries
     & lecture halls
      occupied as they were by losers.

       By November
       she existed on
       other students'
        lecture notes
        in exchange for
      her special popcorn
       which was vegan
     & vaguely Indonesian.

           This worked well for her classmates too—
             the consensus among them
             was that Mina was on the verge of
             a crack-up.

           They could smell it on her.

Mina's Spicy Popcorn

*Buy the freshest organic Native American corn available. Pop half a cup
of it in an air popper. While you're waiting for the corn to pop, stir
together a teaspoon of sriracha, a teaspoon of ground turmeric &
a tablespoon of oil, preferably canola. When the popcorn is done popping,
put it in a large bowl. Pour the oil & spice mixture over it. Toss it together.
Add coarse kosher salt if you need it, but you shouldn't.*

Mina Marches Forth

Home on fall break   the Seven Sisters' Thanksgiving table
thought Mina
was clearly   a desecration
of Native American culture
native American birds
& the cranberry.

Where did Abby stand on this?
How about Malcolm?
Clearly brainwashed. Clearly.

Those women—aunties, *ha!*— understood nothing
of the world outside
the one they'd made
for their children.
They were too busy
serving the meal
washing the dishes
& wrapping up leftovers.

Disgusted with the bourgeois bonds of domesticity
their repetitiveness
& the distinct whiff of subservience
of those so-called radical warrior women

Mina bought herself a pair of boots
(black)   (of repurposed tires)
with $127 she lifted
from Auntie Jean's purse
& marched bravely into her future.

Mina Decides to Become an Artist

Mina had squeezed the lemon of Vassar
          all she could
                    & the fact that no one would room with her
                              —sure, it was a small issue—
                              was a sign she was once again
                                        misunderstood.

It was time for making
          time for gathering
                              into her grasp
                              all the tools of brass & wood
                                        water & bristle
                                        leather & stone
                    that every star of history or
                    the solitary arts was famous for.

                    In a post-Thanksgiving flurry
                                        of repurposing
Mina roasted the bones of a flightless bird
& boiled them with fennel & nutmeg
          down to a rich broth
                    & drank it for courage.

          Broth made from bones is strengthening.

She learned to throw pots
          (& though disappointed there was no *real* throwing)
                    Mina proved an apt potter
                    of pitchers
          with golden glazes
                    until she tired of pottery.

Music
amused her.   But she had the voice of a bullhorn
                              & knew it
                              so she tried the flute
                              & flailed.   & failed.

Then a brush with paint & canvas—
            but the figure escaped her
                    (or rather   the face
                        which always required the same old
                                    four features:
                            eye eye nose mouth)

So she tried still lifes
        & titled them   (because naming, too, is making)
        Citron Feather & Crown
            I II III IV V VI etc...

But in each she saw
an unalterable flaw
        & each one she burned.

                    We destroy what we don't understand
                & hope the fear that accompanies
                    our sense of not-knowing
                            leaves us as well

        —rising like some sort of smoke to some sort of heaven
            where some sort of filter
                recycles it
            for some kind of future.

Once she'd thrown them all into a dented barrel
                & touched   the tongue
                        of a lit match
                        to the corner of the topmost canvas
        Mina watched
                as an eighth-acre of Tyrian purple
                        & yellow ochre
                            curled
                    from the canvases

                    & came
                    at last
                    to life.

Mina Has a Revelation

As she watched the paint darken & lift
ember-edged
into the January sky
Mina understood that she was not
destined
to be an artist.

With this insight
& a vague sense of relief
Mina took a trip back home to New Hampshire
driving her little yolk-colored Subaru
straight through
from Manhattan
past suburbs   sooty cities
over state lines
past a few spectacular glimpses
of the Atlantic &
the scrubby collar of cattails
that filters
the earth from the earth.

A Brief but Eventful Visit Home

The house at the top of the hill
            the house Mina called home
                        looked reassuringly familiar—

                        streaks of pine sap
                                    still ran like honey
                        down the north face of the house
                        & a small gray satellite dish
                                    had replaced the rusty antenna.

    She walked into the kitchen
where a few bushels of bruised & lumpy apples
sat on the cracked linoleum floor
                        & Auntie Anna's canning paraphernalia
                        lay on the table.

                        Auntie Karen tromped up from the basement
                        with a load of wet laundry to be hung.

                        Auntie Anna   Mina was told   was upstairs resting
                                    but Abby would be home soon
                                                from the co-op
                                                    with the groceries.

    That night six aunties squeezed around the stained oak table
                        with their two daughters
                        (auntie Emily had left the year before
                            to pursue her dream:
                        a doctorate in critical theory)
                    reminiscing over bowls of root vegetable stew
                                    & Abby's applesauce
                            when a small
                            purring kitten
                            curled between
                                    Mina's
                        sternum & heart.

Mina slept fitfully
    in the wing chair in the parlor—
        the bedroom she'd shared with Malcolm
            had become Abby's craft room—

    rising before dawn
        to the uneven tock-tock of the mantel clock
        & the intermittent call of a barred owl:

            who cooks for you?
            who cooks for you all?

                She was back
                in Manhattan
                before the
                glass carafe
                had auto-filled
                with coffee.

Discipline in Lemon Chiffon

Once it occurred to her that she was no artist
Mina found time for small pleasures—
                    decorating her apartment
                    & cooking her own meals.
A month of trials & she mastered
        the chard soufflé; two months
    & she'd become a baker
            of gluten-free muffins.

                    But the night
    she learned that Auntie Anna's exhaustion
        was M.S.
        she walked the fifty-nine blocks
                    to Bleecker
    & bought herself two pricey lemon cupcakes
        —Anna's favorite.

            When her headache
            resolved
Mina thought *I can learn to make these.*

Sugar-flour-butter-egg-lemon
            & a pinch of cream of tartar
                to steady
            the delicate crumb.

The ingredients are simple
the discipline difficult.

            Seven weeks
            & then success—
        Mina made something
                to be proud of.

Mina Gets the Mail

Those weeks of culinary experimentation
    left Mina scrambling to cover
            her May obligations.

She found among the bills & catalogues
                    in her post office box
        a letter from Auntie Sarah:

> *Dear M,*
> *Didn't you know this girl?*
> *So sorry. Suicide.*
>   *Your Auntie S.*

        A folded rectangle
        torn from *The Portsmouth Herald*
            fluttered to the floor:

Xia "Ginger" Chew, 20... beloved daughter of Li and Zhu Chu.... departed this earth on April 19...predeceased by her younger brother Ming "Matthew" Chew....who died at the hands of a group of thugs....Ginger is survived by the teens she mentored...

...emigrated from China with her parents as an infant. ...proud graduate of Portsmouth High School.....studying criminal justice at Portsmouth Community College.

A graveside service ....followed by a Celebration... at All Souls Unitarian Universalist... Calling hours will be held from...donations in her memory to The Ginger & Matthew Chew Foundation...consider volunteering....

Some would shake their heads
Some would burst into tears
Some would look upward
Some would collapse

Some would shudder
Some would feel guilt
Some would call the family
Some would wonder if they'd played a part

   Not Mina

   though she wrote a check
   with a note:

      in memory of Ginger.

Love Finds Mina Kali

Look through a telescope   you find galaxies
                          those whirling ellipses held fast
                                        by attraction.

                    But to find love?
          Even a thicket of telescopes
                                   their black legs flamingoed
                                        at the window
              their Galilean monocles
                          are blind to it.

Mina had her share
        of romances—

              a high school steady (five full weeks)
                      with a boy named Om

              winter break with a chain-smoking rugger
                    from Australia or New Zealand
                      she couldn't remember

          & a brutal semester of desk sex
              with an African American assistant professor of art history
              followed by his withdrawal
              of an offer for a grad school recommendation
                  & nine nights
                      of recrimination dreams.

          Men & their half-erect nonsense.

She vowed a year of celibacy
                though   within the span of the moon's wane
                                        love found her
                                        & love fell hard
                          as did Mina   hard
                                        & wholly.

Tricks & Treats

Invited to a Halloween party
at the Park Slope brownstone
         of a famous painter   once Mina's studio art professor
         & her famously wealthy husband
                      (owner of three galleries)
                      (owner of the walls of three galleries)
                      (owner of the art on the walls of three galleries)

Mina   an aspiring fashion designer
                         for a semester
                     went dressed as a canary yellow glowstick.
     A nod to rave culture?
     An homage to trick-or-treaters?
                      She didn't know
                      but she made an impression
                      on the tranny Cleopatra whose diamante diadem
                                     put Liz Taylor to shame
                      & the old fart trying to pass as a hippie.

                         Time for a smoke in the huddle on the deck
                      & yes   the Pleiades were twinkling.

From the shadows   stepped a handsome "soldier"
                      sporting fatigues & a ginger buzz cut:
                         -got an extra?
                         -got a light?
                         -got a name?

          Violet.

          The topaz studs
          in Violet's ears
          winked like
          small cats
          waking.

Here the certain attraction.
Here the flicker of recognition.
Here the bow's draw
                        the sting & ecstatic wound   the hit &
                                                       mutual fall.
Here the *yes*.

Does conversation matter when the meaning was unspoken?

                                        They tapped each other's
                                        contact info
                                        into personal
                                        communication devices
                                        made plans
                                        for brunch the following day.
                                        Made out.

Mina gussied up for brunch
                        pulling on her best black turtleneck
        her near-clean jeans   tucked into black boots
                            (the toes upturned with wear.)

                First to arrive   she smoked a quickie
                                    flicked it
                                    sat
                                    sipped an o.j.

When in walked Violet
        Sergeant Violet
                        in fatigues.
Sometimes a costume is not a
        cool
        ironic
        antiwar statement
                but a uniform worn proudly
                    for service done willingly.

    Mina resisted the urge to bolt
                & holding the plasticized menu like a shield
                        ordered a boiled egg
                    tea   wheat toast
                    with orange marmalade.

She collected herself
                mouthing a silent *what the hell?*
        behind the menu's flimsy cardboard wall
                        took a breath
                        & then met Violet's golden eyes.
                        Mina met the yes in those eyes.

        Over that brunch

over the course
   of a cool November Sunday
      & the weeks that followed
         of the year's shortening wick
            this love was lit.
Mina loves Violet loves Mina

      The eyes of the beloved
       either elevate reflection   or ignore it outright.

    For Mina   they let down that guard
            they tore down her walls
            they invited her to play
 & when she played   too rough
               Violet called her on it.

                Knock it off
                   when Mina leaned over & imitated
                       a server's lisp at the pizza place.
                Knock it off
                   when Mina screamed "asshole" at
                       a passing cabbie who yelled "Dykes!"
                Knock it off
                   When Mina muttered about the mayor
                       the sidewalk garbage, her bakery job.

    Violet had no varnish
       no veneer.

       She was true
          & in being so   loved truly
          as she herself had been loved
          by a widowed father
          never too tired from his third shift
                second job
          to check Violet's homework
          & recite to her in his raspy lilt

the lines he'd been taught
as a child in Kilkenny:

Gently touch a nettle and it'll sting you for your pains
Grasp it as a lad of mettle and soft as silk remains.

She loved Mina with a kind of swaddle
meant at first for babies, cattle.
When Mina tested Violet's mettle
closer holding won the battle.

Mina began to show herself
in fits & starts
worrying that Violet
might turn from her in disgust.
But sooner or later never arrived—
Violet earned Mina's trust.

She loved the 5 year old discouraged from wearing clothes deemed
"too gender-identified"

the 9 year old who asked to learn to cook
& was told she was clumsy

the 13 year old made to stand in the Principal's office
each morning while the other students
recited the Pledge that she'd been taught
was morally wrong.

How to Love a Loaded Gun

A good soldier
knows the
limitations
of her weapons
the right reasons
for their use
& how to
disassemble them.

Domestic Rest

Mina found a small apartment
a few blocks from Westover Air Force base
where Violet was stationed—

the third floor of a narrow but tidy home
owned by a local police officer
& her husband
who despite his disability   (he'd broken his back in a fall
at the ironworks in Bath)
helped Mina push a dusty four-piece sectional
she'd found in the dumpster
out behind the pink brick medical building
(some habits can't be broken)

up up up three flights of stairs
to the square living room with its western view
of the base
& the Berkshires.

The Kims were happy
to have   not only her rent
but the scent
of Mina's culinary experiments
on the harvest gold 70's era stove
which ranged
from beet soup to banana pudding to *bi bim bap*
the last
a bit worrisome
being a Korean dish
& thus potentially politically inappropriate
but Violet reassured Mina
it's enjoyed on both sides of the DMZ.

Mina's Golden Beet Soup

Choose ten taut golden beets. Wash them, then trim their green tresses & set them aside for a salad. Peel your beets, then chop them into small cubes. Do the same to two yellow onions. Cut from a hand of fresh ginger root a piece the size of the tip of your thumb. Peel & chop this very finely. Take an orange & grate all its fragrant peel into a small pile of filament.

Now set a large pot over the flame on your stove & melt a half stick of sweet butter. Scoop all you've chopped & grated into the pot. Cover the pot & let it simmer, stirring every few minutes, for a quarter hour. Pour in seven cups or more of chicken broth. Add the juice of that orange whose peel you've grated. Cover the pot again & let it simmer for an hour. Then let the mixture rest uncovered to cool.

Whir a ladle or two at a time in a food processor until it's velvet smooth. Add a teaspoon of cider vinegar & a pinch of cayenne. Taste your soup for need of salt & pepper. Return it to the pot and heat it gently.

This Should Have Been a Honeymoon

Each month
their life on the third floor of the
                    narrow house
                        grew a bit
      easier   as Mina & Violet settled into a routine.

Once Violet left for her job on the base
where she worked as a logistics officer
Mina would sit at the small table
they'd bought at a yard sale
& with a cup of milky tea at her elbow
she'd make a list
                  of things that needed doing: *clean bathroom*
                                                        pay water bill
                                                        co-op volunteer day
                                                        buy bones for soup

        This arrangement
      —Mina in charge of the house while Violet worked—
                became their private joke
      —so much for degendering their household tasks—

          Why don't we make it official & get married?
                said Violet one April morning
                    as she brushed a dusting of snow
                from the bedroom windowsill
                    before topping off the bird feeder.

Mina smiled
adding it to her list: *get married*
but Violet persisted, *I'm not kidding.*

                        Violet had just received orders
                            for redeployment.
                        Having served in Korea
                        & briefly in Iraq   she sensed
                            that a tour in Afghanistan
        (some of the troops were calling it "Operation Enduring Operation")

would be her toughest.

All summer & through the fall
Mina & Violet spent their days
                    in the kind of cram-it-all-in busyness
              well-known to members of the Armed Forces
                  on the threshold of deployment.

Violet cajoled & cajoled & cajoled
        laying out the case for marriage
        but Mina would have none of it:

                              Marriage is the licensing
                                        of private life.

                      We must fight to maintain our freedom!
                      Separation of church & state.
                      There should be some kind of partition
                                some kind of wall...

              Oh.

On December 4th
three days after the President announced
a troop surge   of thirty thousand
Violet was deployed to Afghanistan.

              On December 13
after less than two weeks in Afghanistan
Violet was killed.

Two Officers at the Door

Two officers at the door.

Something about a convoy
an IED

something about immediately

no suffering

Mina Alone

All right   *All right*   *All right*

Mina murmured again & again
        as she spooned up a bit of rice
        from the little pot
        Mrs. Kim had left on her doorstep

        as she turned off the shower & reached
        for the yellow towel   one of the pair
        that she & Violet had bought at the PX
        during their last shopping trip. *All right*

        All right   *All right*
        as she gasped at the towel's rough embrace
        Her skin hurt.   *All right*

    All right   on Christmas eve
    All right   on Christmas day
    All right   on New Year's eve
    All right   on New Year's day
    All right   on Wednesday Thursday Friday Saturday
                    Sunday Monday Tuesday
    All right   another week & yet another

        Five months of *all rights*
          then Mina dialed the phone
            that rang in the kitchen
              of a small house in Portsmouth

        Hello? said Mina,   *Hello?*

Cast Out from the Pleiades

—*Well hello. It's been quite a while since we've talked. No you can't speak to Auntie Anna. Why? Because Auntie Nan drove her to the doctor. She's not doing well, Mina. I've had to step in and take care of the cooking. And the shopping. And the laundry after Auntie Karen separated her shoulder. Yes, she slipped on the ice. Months ago. Of course Malcolm's been helping. Well I'm very sorry to hear your news. I liked Violet, but things here are so chaotic that I don't think it's a good idea for you to come back to Portsmouth. I've got everything under control. Yeah, you too. Bye.*

Coda

The way of grief's the closing of a shutter
a camera obscura; a galaxy
of pinhole truths revealed, likenesses subtler
than the stars. Out from the Pleiades
our Mina wandered, out from the boundaries
of righteous dogma she had mined for malice.
That she'd found passion almost undid Abby
who found herself at thirty—nursemaid, manless.

The good can flounder. Who said the world was just?
The lens has cast it image upside down
but accurately—no detail's lost.
Perhaps what's gone around has come around.
A cruelty like Mina's was only—& best
tempered by her love for Violet.

Notes

"Gently touch a nettle and it'll sting you for your pains
  Grasp it as a lad of mettle and soft as silk remains."
                    —Sixteenth century English proverb

References are made to the song "Another Brick in the Wall (Part II)" by Pink Floyd.

"Galilean monocles" refers to the fact that Galileo invented the telescope.

On December 1st, 2009, President Barack Obama ordered a controversial "troop surge" of thirty thousand American soldiers into Afghanistan.

Matthew Chew was a young artist jumped by a group of six young men on the evening of October 29th, 2010 in New London, CT as he walked home from his job at a pizzeria. He was stabbed to death.

Ginger Chews are a popular sweet and the winner of Fiery Food Association's Scovie Award for Best Candy.

About the Author

Leslie McGrath's interviews with poets appear regularly in *The Writer's Chronicle*. Winner of the 2004 Pablo Neruda Prize for poetry, she is the author of *Opulent Hunger, Opulent Rage* (2009), a poetry collection, and two chapbooks: *Toward Anguish* (2007) and *By the Windpipe* (2014.) Her poems have appeared in *The Awl, Agni, The Common, Slate*, and elsewhere. She teaches creative writing and literature at Central Connecticut State University, and is series editor of The Tenth Gate, a new poetry imprint of The Word Works press.